TINY HOUSE,
BIG FIX

TINY HOUSE, BIG FIX

GAIL ANDERSON-DARGATZ

ORCA BOOK PUBLISHERS

Library and Archives Canada Cataloguing in Publication

Anderson-Dargatz, Gail, 1963–, author
Tiny house, big fix / Gail Anderson-Dargatz.
(Rapid reads)

Issued in print and electronic formats.
ISBN 978-1-4598-2118-7 (softcover).—ISBN 978-1-4598-2119-4 (PDF).—
ISBN 978-1-4598-2120-0 (EPUB)

I. Title. II. Series: Rapid reads
PS8551.N3574T56 2019   C813'.54   C2018-904896-4
C2018-904897-2

First published in the United States, 2019
Library of Congress Control Number: 2018954090

Summary: In this short novel, a single mother and her
daughters have a hard time finding a home. (RL 3.3)

*Orca Book Publishers is dedicated to preserving the environment and
has printed this book on Forest Stewardship Council® certified paper.*

Orca Book Publishers gratefully acknowledges the support for
its publishing programs provided by the following agencies: the Government
of Canada, the Canada Council for the Arts and the Province of British Columbia
through the BC Arts Council and the Book Publishing Tax Credit.

Cover images by shutterstock.com/Gajus

ORCA BOOK PUBLISHERS
orcabook.com

Printed and bound in Canada.

22 21 20 19 • 4 3 2 1

For Hadarah, who inspires me daily

ONE

AS LIAM AND I built the interior wall frame, it lay flat on the first floor of the unfinished house. I hammered in the last nail to hold a stud in place, then put down my nail gun and stretched my back. I'd spent a lot of my day bent over as I banged walls together, and my back was sore. The house had no roof yet, only framed-in exterior walls. We were both sweaty and grubby from working under the sun all day. I'd kept my mess of curls pulled back into a ponytail to keep the hair off my face. I wasn't sure whether Liam had bothered to comb his hair. Now, toward the end of our shift, his dark mop stood up at all angles.

"Ready, Sadie?" he asked. I nodded. Together, we raised the interior wall frame we had just built and kicked it into place. We both knew what we needed to do, so we didn't talk much. Liam and I had been on the job together for several months. I found him easy to work with.

Most people are surprised when I tell them I'm a carpenter, working as a framer in housing construction. Not many women work in the trade, even now that skilled carpenters and framers are in short supply. But building is in my blood. My dad owned a small construction company until he passed away. He taught me how to use power tools when I was just a kid. I built my own go-cart and tree fort when I was ten.

When I was a teen, I worked summers alongside Dad, framing houses. In fact, I worked part-time for my dad even after I married. I quit when I got pregnant with Zoe. Then I had Maggie not long after. I was a stay-at-home mom for nearly fifteen years. But when I divorced, I needed to make a decent living for the kids and me. A career in construction seemed like the natural choice.

As I worked with Liam to nail the wall into place, I felt my cell buzz in my jean pocket. I finished my task before checking my phone. There was a text from my youngest daughter. **Mom**, it read. **You've got to come get me!**

"Damn," I said.

"Something wrong, Sadie?" Liam asked.

I scrolled through my messages as I spoke. "Maggie is still waiting outside the school. Zoe should have picked her up half an hour ago." I read another panicked text from Maggie. "And she's freaking out."

My youngest daughter, Maggie, goes to the rural elementary school near our village. My oldest, Zoe, attends the junior high school in town. Maggie is nine, but I don't feel she is ready to walk home alone. She would have to cross a busy highway to get there.

Instead, Maggie hangs out at the playground at her school with other kids until Zoe's bus arrives. Then Zoe walks her home.

I replied to Maggie. **Just hang on, sweetheart. I'll find out what's going on.**

I quickly texted my oldest daughter. **Where are you? Maggie is at school, waiting. She's scared.**

"Hey!" my crew boss yelled at me from the other side of the house. He was nailing together a short wall frame on what would be the bathroom. "Use that damn phone on your own time. When you're on the clock, all I want to see are your elbows and butt." It was something Bruce always said. He meant he wanted to see us working, bent over and swinging our hammers.

"Yeah, yeah," I called back as I pocketed my phone.

Then Liam and I started laying out the studs for the next wall. Once that was done, I banged in the first stud on the new section of wall with a framing nailer. Liam worked on the other side of the frame, nailing in studs with his nail gun.

As I moved on to the next stud, I felt my phone buzz again. I glanced over to make sure Bruce wasn't watching and checked my messages. There was another from Maggie, wondering if her sister was okay. But there was nothing from Zoe yet. I sent another text to my oldest daughter. **Zoe, where are you?**

Liam straightened up with his nail gun in hand. "Maggie still freaking out?" he asked.

Liam had kids too. We often talked about parenting during our lunch breaks. He knew all about the problems I was dealing with.

"I'm starting to worry too," I said.

"Oh, I wouldn't fret," said Liam. "When my boys stay with me, they're always running off with the local kids. I don't know where they are half the time. That's a good thing too. Kids need to explore the world on their own."

He fixed another stud in place with the nail gun. *Zap. Zap.* "I'm sure Zoe is just hanging out with friends after school," he said.

"I hope so," I said.

I messaged Zoe yet again. **Answer me!**

Bruce yelled, "Sadie, get to work!"

I rolled my eyes at Liam. "Bruce is such a slave driver," I said. I didn't know whether to love my crew boss or hate him. Liam only grinned.

I set my phone in front of me as I bent to

nail in the studs. As I worked, I kept peeking at my cell to see if Zoe had replied. I was relieved when she finally texted back. **Chill, Mom. I'm fine. I met up with Jason and lost track of time. But I missed my bus. Pick me up?**

I swore under my breath.

"What now?" asked Liam.

"Zoe," I said, throwing up a hand. "I have to drive all the way into town to pick her up."

"She missed her bus again? That's the second time this week."

"And it's only the first week of school," I said. "I have to put an end to this before it becomes a habit."

Stay at school, I texted Zoe. **I'll get Maggie and meet you there.**

Then I sent another message to my youngest daughter. **I'll pick you up soon, honey. Just wait outside the school. Zoe is fine.**

Bruce called out, "Sadie, what did I just tell you about using that phone on my time?"

"Okay, okay," I said.

But just then my phone rang. With Bruce watching, I answered without checking who was calling. "What is it *now?*" I asked, thinking Zoe was on the line.

"Sadie?" the caller asked. It was a woman's voice.

"Sorry. Yes, this is Sadie." I laughed a little in embarrassment as I glanced over at my boss. "I thought my daughter was calling."

"This is Ruby," the caller said.

Ruby? It took me a moment to realize who it was. My landlady. I hardly ever saw her. I mailed my rent checks to her each month. The only times I talked to her were when the dryer stopped working and there was a leak in the roof. Even then it was only to get her okay to fix the problems myself.

"Sorry, yes, Ruby," I said. "What can I do for you?"

"I'm hoping to swing by your place this evening." She paused. "We need to talk."

"Is something wrong?" I asked. I lowered my voice. "You received this month's rent payment, didn't you? I know I mailed it."

"Yes, yes," said Ruby. "You're always on time with your rent. And whenever I drive by, the place looks tidy. I don't feel I have to check in on you. You're the best renter I've ever had."

"Then what is it? Should I be worried?"

She cleared her throat. "I think we better talk face-to-face."

"I'm just leaving work to pick up my daughters," I said. "I have to run into town. But we should be back home by six."

"I'll stop in just after supper then."

"Sure," I said. "See you later."

After we'd hung up I stared at the phone

a moment. Ruby had been pleasant enough. But a sick feeling was creeping into my stomach, like something was about to go terribly wrong.

TWO

LIAM PUT DOWN his nailer and stepped around the wall frame to talk to me. "Everything okay?" he asked. "You look like you just got some bad news."

"I'm not sure." I pocketed my phone. "My landlady wants to see me. I guess I'll find out why this evening. But right now I've got to pick up my kids."

"You're not leaving work early again, are you?" my crew boss asked.

Bruce was a big meaty guy with a

shaved head. Even his scalp turned red when he was angry. Or maybe he was just sunburned. Even though I was wearing sunscreen, I could feel the sunburn on my own cheeks. As a redhead, I burn easily. Zoe keeps bugging me to wear a hat at work.

"Sorry, Bruce," I said. "I've got one scared kid crying at her school and another stranded in town."

"Zoe missed her bus again?" he asked. "Are you kidding me?"

"I don't know what to do with her," I said. "She's been acting out for months now. Talking back, slamming doors, and now she's missing the bus on purpose."

"She's what, fourteen?" Bruce asked. "Kids are all drama queens at that age. Sometimes it seems like they're only able to think about themselves."

I imagined he spoke from experience. He'd raised a couple of teenage daughters himself.

"It's just a stage," Liam added. "Zoe will outgrow it."

"I hope so." I wiped the sweat from my forehead with the back of my hand. "It seems like teens take more work than toddlers. At least, my Zoe does. And that's energy I don't have right now, working this much. I think she may be missing the bus just to get my attention."

Bruce shook his head, dismissing my comment. "The girl's got to learn you can't keep running off to pick her up. I say make her wait until your shift is over. Teach her a lesson. In any case, I need you here."

"What do you expect me to do?" I asked him. "Make my nine-year-old wait at the school alone for hours, crying? I don't have anyone I can call to pick her up."

Bruce held up a hand to stop me from going further. "I get it," he said. "I have kids too, remember." He rubbed his chin, leaving a streak of dirt there. "All I'm saying is, you've got to pull things together on the home front so you can get your work done. Over the summer you skipped out because Zoe left Maggie at home alone. Now that they're back at school, you're running off because Zoe missed the bus. The kid is thoughtless."

I shook my head. "That's not true. Zoe *is* acting out. But she's doing that because I'm not around enough. And I know I depend on her too much. She shouldn't have to take care of Maggie all the time. Zoe makes dinners too. She takes care of the laundry and cleans up the house. It's too big a load for a kid that age."

"That's not so bad," said Liam. "Chores are good for kids."

"I guess. But all that doesn't leave much time for hanging out with her friends. She's started to resent everything I ask her to do.

I don't blame her. I just wish I could afford to be home more, like I was before the divorce. With all the overtime we've been pulling, this job isn't exactly family friendly."

"Not my problem," said Bruce. "We build houses when we get a contract and the weather's good. You're here to work. You can't leave early day after day and expect to keep your job."

My phone buzzed yet again, and I checked my messages. There was another text from Maggie. **Are you coming? Everybody is gone!**

On my way, honey! I replied, typing with my thumbs.

"Are you listening to me?" Bruce asked.

"There's a shortage of framers," I said, adjusting my tool belt. "You really think you can replace me that easily?"

"I just hired Alice, didn't I?" Bruce waved at our coworker. Wearing a red bandanna, Alice was hard at work off to the side of the unfinished house. She had her head down, cutting a stud to fit a window opening.

I had talked Bruce into hiring another woman for the framing crew. He'd chosen Alice because she had taken a carpentry course at the local college. Now she continued to learn on the job as an apprentice. And we'd already become friends. Alice, Liam and I ate lunch together every day and sometimes hung out together at my place after work.

"You're a good framer, Sadie," Bruce said. "I don't want to lose you. But I need people I can count on. With you gone for the rest of the day, it's going to take Liam longer to finish the job. I can't afford to keep you on if you cost me money."

Crap. I didn't want to lose this job. Especially over Zoe missing her bus.

"Of course," I said, nodding. "You're right. I won't let it happen again." I put my phone in my pocket. "I'll come in early Monday morning to make up for it, okay?"

Bruce dismissed me with a wave and went back to work.

I glanced back at Liam, hoping for his support. "Bruce, eh?" I said. "Always getting himself worked up. He's going to give himself a stroke."

But Liam only shrugged. "I'm not too thrilled about you leaving early either," he said. "Without you here, I'll be putting up these walls by myself for the rest of the day. It's a two-person job."

"Bruce is here. And Alice can help."

"Bruce has his own work to do. And I have to tell Alice how to do everything."

"She'll be fine," I said. "She's catching on." I picked my way through the boards on the floor, heading for the ladder. I called over my shoulder, "And I'll find a way to make it up to you." At that moment I was thinking

I'd buy him a six-pack of beer. But he had something else in mind.

"So you *will* bring the kids over to my house Sunday?" he asked.

Oops! I'd walked right into that one. The day before, Liam had asked me over for dinner. I hadn't given him an answer. I wasn't sure if he was asking me on a date or not. It didn't seem like one, not when I had two kids in tow. But what if it was?

I turned back to Liam. He looked at me hopefully, like a dog in a pet-shop window. "I'm not sure," I said, thinking of my landlady's call. "I'll have to see how the weekend goes. It's already off to a rocky start."

"Yeah, sure," he said. Then he perked up. "Your girls would really like my house. Honestly. My own boys love it."

I laughed. "Your house? What's so special about your house?"

"You'll see. So are you coming?"

"Look, Liam—" My phone buzzed again, and I read the text. Maggie was wondering why I was taking so long to get there.

"You can bring dessert," Liam said. "Maybe you can make a batch of those great brownies you brought to work that one day."

Then Zoe texted again, saying she was going to the mall with Jason. She wanted to meet me there. *Ugh.* I didn't want to search the mall for my teenage daughter. And who the hell was Jason?

I quickly texted her. **I said wait for me at the school!**

"Did you hear me, Sadie?" Liam asked. "You okay bringing dessert?"

"Yeah, I heard you," I said, still checking my phone. "Brownies. But right now, I have to go."

"It's a date then?" Liam asked, sounding doubtful. "Will I see you Sunday?"

I hesitated. So this *was* a date? I knew

I had to set Liam straight. I just didn't think of him in a romantic way. We were work buddies, friends. Nothing more. Still, I didn't want to hurt his feelings either, especially not with Bruce listening in. "I'll text you over the weekend," I said. "I'll let you know whether I'm coming or not then. Okay?"

My phone buzzed yet again as Maggie sent another message. I quickly texted her back. **On my way!**

"Sorry, Liam," I said. "I really have to go."

THREE

I PARKED THE TRUCK in front of Maggie's school. Aside from the gym and office, the building was made up of a line of classrooms. Each class had its own outside door, like in a strip mall.

The buses, parents and teachers were long gone. My daughter sat alone on the outside steps of her classroom, hugging her knees. Even when Maggie was in a crowd of other kids, she was easy to spot. Taking after me, she had an unruly mop of bright-red curls.

Anyone could tell she was my daughter. Now that I worked in construction, she'd even started dressing down like me, in jeans and T-shirts.

"What took you so long?" she sobbed as I got out of the truck. Her freckled face was red from crying.

I wrapped my arm around her. "I got here as quickly as I could," I said. "But I had to drive from my job site, honey. That took a little while."

"Everybody left," she said. "Even the principal's gone. My teacher had to stay and watch me."

She pointed to the classroom window. Her teacher gave me a stern look before disappearing into the room. That's just great, I thought. We hadn't even had "meet the teacher" night, and the woman already had a bad impression of me.

I wiped the tears from Maggie's cheeks.

"I'm so sorry you had to wait, baby," I said. "But there's nothing to worry about. Zoe just missed her bus again. Now we have to drive into town and pick her up. You know what *that* means, don't you?" I grinned.

Her face brightened. "We get pizza for supper!"

"You got that right!" We always stop for pizza on our way home from our weekly shopping trip into town. When I'd picked up Zoe at her school earlier that week, we'd bought pizza then too. It occurred to me that maybe this wasn't the best parenting move. Was *pizza* one of the reasons Zoe was missing her bus again?

But on second thought, I doubted it. Aside from getting my attention, I suspected her new friend Jason was the real reason she'd stayed in town.

"Okay," I said to Maggie. "Grab your stuff and jump in the truck."

"Can I ride in the front?" Maggie asked as she picked up her backpack. "On the way home from town too?"

"You sure can." I would make Zoe sit in the back seat of the crew cab on the way home. As the oldest, she usually sat in the front. Not this time. Not after missing the bus and making me drive all the way into town.

"Buckle up," I told Maggie as she got in the truck.

I pulled onto the highway to head into town, passing through our village. Our little town is a tourist spot, on the edge of the lake. In the summer, city people flock here from all over. Many of them own cottages along the beach.

The summer people come for the water and sandy shoreline, but also for the surrounding landscape. My drive into town follows the lake through lovely rolling hills.

Vineyards grow on many of them. There are a lot of wineries in the area.

But I wasn't in a mood to enjoy the beauty this day. Now that I had time to think, I fretted about my landlady's call. If Ruby wanted to talk to me in person, I figured she must want to raise the rent.

I knew rental prices had gone way up. There was a housing shortage in the area because so many people had moved here for work. They were buying and renting homes, and that was pushing up both housing prices and rent. More and more people were building homes too. That was good for Bruce's construction business and meant steady work for me. But I knew many families were having a hard time finding affordable places to live. If Ruby wanted to raise my rent, I wasn't sure how I would make ends meet. I pretty much used up each month's pay as it was. My ex-husband, Kevin, did pay child support. But that small monthly amount didn't go far.

"You okay, Mommy?" Maggie asked as we stopped at the first traffic light in town. "Is something wrong? You look so sad." My youngest daughter always picks up on my mood.

"I'm fine," I said. I smoothed her wild red hair as we waited for the light to turn green. "I'm just tired. Everything's good." I put on a smile for her sake.

As I drove into the high school parking lot, I was surprised to find Zoe actually there. She had been acting out so much lately. I'd thought she might go to the mall even though I'd told her to wait at the school. But there she was, sitting on the front steps with a skinny, blue-haired boy. Jason, I imagined.

As soon as I pulled up to the curb, the boy slunk off like he was afraid to meet me. So, I thought, Jason isn't just a friend. Zoe, my little girl, had a *boyfriend* already.

I studied my oldest daughter as she picked up her backpack. Almost over-night she'd grown up. Zoe is more like my husband, tall and lean. Her hair is darker than mine, a reddish brown. While Maggie and I let our hair grow wild, Zoe insists on stylish cuts.

She dresses far better than Maggie and me too. Today she wore jeans, but hers had flared legs with hummingbirds embroidered on them. Her lace blouse had bell sleeves, and her curls were tamed with a scarf.

Zoe opened the front passenger door. "Took you long enough," she said. Then she gave me the stink eye. "I've been waiting, like, *forever*. Why didn't you let me hang out at the mall with Jason?"

"Don't talk to me like that, young lady," I said. "And you have some nerve complaining. I had to leave work early and drive all the way into town just because you missed your bus. And I know you missed it on purpose. You just wanted to spend more time with that boy."

"His name is Jason." Zoe didn't bother to argue further. I was clearly right. She *had* purposefully missed her bus. Instead, she punched Maggie's arm. "Get out of my seat, munchkin."

"*Zoe*," I said, warning her.

"Ow!" Maggie complained, though I knew it didn't really hurt. She pushed Zoe back from the door with both hands. "Get out of here. Mom said I could ride in the front."

"I *never* ride in the back," Zoe said. She sniffed like that was beneath her.

"You are today," I said firmly. "Get in the back."

"But—"

I held up my hand to stop her from saying anything more. In response, she slammed the front door shut. Then she yanked open the back door of the crew cab and threw her backpack inside. "This sucks," she said as she got in. "I've got, like, zero legroom."

"Maybe next time you'll think twice about missing the bus." I turned to face her. "This has got to stop, Zoe. My boss told me I could lose my job if I keep leaving work early. And I can't afford the gas for all these useless trips."

Zoe slumped in her seat. "*Whatever*," she mumbled. But her pale cheeks grew blotchy like they always do when she is upset or embarrassed. She knew she'd messed up.

As I pulled onto the highway Zoe caught my eye in the mirror. "Pizza for supper?" she asked hopefully. "I promise I won't miss the bus again." Then she offered me a sheepish grin that lit up her pretty face.

I shook my head and smiled despite myself. I knew that was the closest my daughter would come to saying she was sorry.

"Yeah," I said. "We'll stop for pizza."

FOUR

MY LANDLADY, Ruby, was waiting on the deck of our rental when we finally got home. The house was a small bungalow with cedar siding. Nothing much to look at, not like the home I'd lost through the divorce.

The house I once owned with my ex-husband is a two-story Edwardian-era building. I did a lot of renos on our old place. But we'd had to take out loans to do the work. When we sold the house, the bank still owned most of it.

I'd loved our old place, and I knew the girls had too. It was a real step down to move from that great home into this rental. But the bungalow was close to Maggie's school and on a quiet rural road. It came with a good-sized yard with fruit trees.

There was also room to park our travel trailer. That travel trailer was the one thing I'd insisted on keeping during the divorce, and my ex-husband agreed. It was old, and the roof leaked, so it wasn't worth much. But the kids had good memories of camping in it. We still used it now and again, for getting away on weekends.

After we got out of the truck, Ruby said hello to the girls. Then Zoe carried the box of leftover pizza into the house, and Maggie followed. I invited Ruby inside, but she shook her head. "Let's talk out here," she said. She glanced at the girls before they closed the door.

So she didn't want them hearing our conversation.

"What's this about?" I asked.

"You may have read there's a housing crisis in the area," she said. "Housing prices are going through the roof. No pun intended." She smiled a little. "People are having trouble finding places to live."

"You're going to raise our rent, aren't you?"

"I'm afraid it's worse than that," she said.

My voice rose in panic. "You're selling this house?"

She shook her head. "No, I'm keeping the place. But my daughter and her family are moving back into the area. My son-in-law found work here. He starts this week, as a matter of fact. I'm thrilled, of course. But—"

"But they haven't found a place to live."

Ruby nodded. "And my daughter is expecting. She's due to have her baby the second week in October. They already have two toddlers, twins. Things are rather desperate for them. They need a place to live, *now*."

I felt my stomach sink. "You've offered them this house."

"Yes."

"But *we* need the place!" I cried. "You're asking us to move? What are *we* supposed to do?" When I saw the shocked expression on her face, I took a deep breath to calm my anger. "I'm sorry about my outburst. It's just...you said I was the best renter you'd ever had. You have no reason to kick us out. No legal reason."

"I know. But my daughter is pregnant. And family comes first. You must understand."

"Can't your family stay with you until they find something?"

"The house you're living in now was the

one I shared with my husband. When he died, I moved into a one-bedroom seniors' apartment in town. There simply isn't room at my place for my daughter, her husband and her kids. They would have no place to sleep."

I sighed. "I understand," I said. "I'll start searching for another place. We'll be out before November."

"I need you out of the house before October first."

"October first! But that's less than a month from now. You're supposed to give us two months' notice."

"My daughter doesn't have two months." Ruby held out both hands, pleading. "As it is, I've given you more time than we can afford. Think about it from our point of view. My daughter will have to move and then have a baby, all within two weeks. And she has the twins to worry about."

"Ruby, I need more time to find a place for *my* kids. As you just said, there's a housing crisis."

"I'm sorry, Sadie. I wish I didn't have to ask you to move. But I've got to look out for my daughter and her family."

"I'm within my rights to file a complaint, you know."

"I hope you won't make an issue out of it. That would only lead to bad feelings all around. You can hardly expect a pregnant mother to go without a home."

"Of course not," I said. "But you've put me in an impossible position."

"My daughter is in a bad place too. Don't blame me. Blame the housing shortage."

"Okay," I said, resigned. "We'll be out of here by the end of the month."

"Thanks, Sadie."

Just then I saw Maggie, watching us from behind the screen of the kitchen window.

Zoe stood behind her. We'd left that window wide open.

Ruby followed my gaze until she saw the girls. "Well, I'll leave you to pass on the news," she said. But I knew I didn't have to. My daughters had heard every word Ruby and I had said.

I raked my hands through my hair as I watched Ruby drive away. Maggie ran out and wrapped her arms around my waist. I hugged her back. Zoe followed, with our cat, Mr. Snuggles, trailing behind.

"Well, that sucks," Zoe said.

I nodded. "Yes, it does."

"You should fight it," said Zoe. "Like you said, file a complaint or something."

"Yes, but what's the point?" I asked. "You heard Ruby. Her daughter is expecting a baby. And she has young children. This is Ruby's house, after all. She has every right to offer it to her daughter."

"You said she's supposed to give us two months' notice."

"Yes, she is. But I don't feel good about making things harder on a pregnant mom. With a move ahead of her, she's already under enough stress as it is. We'll just have to find another place to live."

"Where?" Maggie asked.

"I'm not sure yet, honey. But we'll figure something out."

"Can I take my tree fort to our new place?" Maggie asked.

I glanced over at the platform in the crook of the old Manitoba maple. Maggie and I had built that tree fort together. I make a point of teaching my girls building skills. Zoe isn't really into it, but Maggie enjoys working with her hands. I can see her going into the trades when she is older.

"We'll leave the fort for the kids who are about to move in here," I said. "They'll love it."

"But it's *my* tree fort! I built it!"

"We can't take it with us, honey." I tried to smile as I stated the obvious. "The tree has to stay here."

"What about Mr. Snuggles?" Maggie asked.

I bent to scratch the cat's head. "We won't leave our kitty behind," I said. "He's family."

Zoe picked up Mr. Snuggles, cuddling the cat. "I don't want to move again," said Zoe. "I still miss our old house."

"I do too," I said. "And I don't want to move either. I thought we'd be here for a while."

"It's okay, Mom," Maggie said. Then she echoed me. "We'll figure something out."

"You got that right," I said. "We'll find a place, even if we have to move to a new community."

Maggie looked panicked, as if she might cry. "I don't want to leave my school."

"And I'm not leaving my friends."

"You mean you're not leaving Jason, your *boyfriend*," said Maggie.

"Shut up," said Zoe.

"You shut up," said Maggie.

Zoe dropped Mr. Snuggles to the ground, and the cat charged off. "Why did you and Dad have to get divorced anyway?" Zoe asked me. "You ruined *everything*."

I didn't know what to say to that. My marriage had ended when my husband had an affair. It hurt to think Zoe blamed *me* for the divorce. I put my hand over my mouth as I blinked away the tears.

Maggie hugged me again. "You're making Mom cry," she told Zoe.

Zoe growled in frustration as she marched into the house. She slammed the kitchen door shut behind her.

"You okay, Mom?" Maggie asked.

"Oh, honey," I said, wiping my eyes.

"I'm the one who should be asking that."

"We'll be fine, right?"

"Yes, we'll be just fine." But my voice trembled a little as I said it, betraying me. I wasn't sure of anything in that moment. Still, I put on a brave face and took her hand. "We had our pizza. How about we have some ice cream for dessert?"

Maggie jumped in excitement. "Ice cream!" she shouted, as if that would make everything better.

FIVE

I SPENT SATURDAY and Sunday searching online for places to rent. I quickly realized houses were now out of my budget range. And most of the apartments I phoned about were already taken. I took the kids to see the remaining rentals in our village. Most had already been scooped up by the time we got there. Others turned out to be more than I could afford.

By Sunday afternoon it had become clear we would have to find a place outside

our village. We might have to move into town—
if we could find a place there. I didn't tell
Maggie that yet though. She would be heart-
broken to hear she'd have to switch schools.

As the dinner hour neared, I sat back
from my laptop and rubbed my eyes. I was
exhausted from hunting for a place to rent.
The last thing I wanted to do was make
supper. Then, at that thought, I remembered
Liam's dinner invitation. *Crap!* I'd forgotten
to text him.

If I didn't bother to call or turned him
down, I knew he'd feel rejected. But if I went
to his place for dinner, I knew I'd have to
make it clear I wasn't interested in dating
him. Working with Liam after this would be
awkward either way. I sighed. I knew I had
to get it over with.

I texted Liam. **You still into having us
over for dinner tonight?**

He messaged back right away, like he'd

been waiting for my text. **Yes! Come over anytime!**

"Hey, girls," I called from the kitchen table.

Maggie was in her room, watching cartoons on Netflix on her tablet. Zoe was in her room too, doing homework on her laptop. She was probably also listening to music and texting her friends at the same time. We seemed to spend so much of our evenings and weekends in separate rooms these days.

"Are you guys into going over to Liam's this evening?" I called.

When neither of the girls answered right away, I added, "He's offered to barbecue burgers for us."

"Burgers!" Maggie shouted. I took that as a yes.

Zoe wandered into the kitchen, texting on her phone. Mr. Snuggles wrapped himself around her leg. "What was that?" she asked. She kept her eyes on her cell.

"We're having burgers at Liam's place," I said. "Want to come?"

She shrugged. "I guess." Then she looked up. "Wait, is this a date? I mean, are you and Liam a thing now?"

I shook my head as I texted Liam, asking for his address. "No date." Not for me, in any case. Liam thought it *was* a date though. There had to be a way to let him down easy.

I thought about that for a minute, and then I sent another message to our new framer, Alice. **Into a BBQ at Liam's tonight?**

Alice, Liam and I already hung out a lot together. I figured if I brought Alice along now, Liam would know I didn't see this dinner as a date. Maybe I wouldn't have to face him about the issue at all.

Alice immediately texted back, **I'm in! Where does he live?**

How about I pick you up on the way? I'd been to her apartment a few times. She lived right in the heart of our village.

She messaged right back. **I'll be waiting outside.**

See you at five.

I dug through my closet for a summer dress and sandals. Then I took the time to put on makeup and arrange my hair around my shoulders. I slipped on hoop earrings and a matching silver necklace and stepped back to inspect myself in the mirror. I hadn't worn a dress in ages. It looked good on me.

When I came out of my room, both of my girls seemed shocked. "Mommy!" cried Maggie. "You're wearing a dress!"

I smiled. "I guess it has been a while."

Maggie crossed her arms and frowned at me. "You said this wasn't a date. You said Liam and you aren't a *thing*."

I smiled a little at Maggie's use of her

older sister's slang. "It's not. We're not."

"Then why are you all dressed up?"

It was a good question. If this wasn't a date with Liam, why had I bothered to put on a dress? I didn't have an answer to that, even for myself.

"I think you look nice," said Zoe. Then she nudged Maggie to get her to stop being rude. "*Doesn't* she?"

"Yeah, you look pretty, Mom."

"Why, thank you."

On our way to pick up Alice, the girls and I stopped at the small local grocery for some two-bite brownies. As an afterthought, I picked up a six-pack of beer for Liam. I had left work early on Friday, leaving him short-handed. I owed him one. And a beer might soften the blow when he realized I wasn't into dating him.

From the store I drove across the highway to pick up Alice. She lived in an apartment above the drugstore in our village and was waiting outside as promised. She jumped into the front of the truck as Zoe climbed in the back with Maggie. Alice was dressed casually, in jeans and a red T-shirt. Her hair was pulled back under a bandanna, just like she wore it at work.

"Wow," she said, scanning my dress. "Look at you! You clean up good."

I shrugged off the attention. Then, as we drove to Liam's, I told Alice about my problem finding a place to rent.

"If you need to, you can stay in my apartment," Alice said. "Until something turns up. I have two bedrooms. The second bedroom is set up as an office right now, but I hardly ever use it."

I shook my head. "Zoe, Maggie and I would have to sleep in one room. We need more space than that. We'd drive each other crazy and take you along with us."

Zoe snorted. "You can say that again. No way I'm sleeping in the same room as her." She pointed a thumb at her sister. "She snores."

"Hey!" Maggie said. "You're the one who snores."

"You do!"

"No, *you* do."

"That's enough, girls," I said, eyeing them through the rear-view mirror. They had just proven my point. We *would* drive each other nuts. "Thanks for the offer," I told Alice. "But honestly, I just couldn't do that to you." Or myself, I thought.

She shrugged. "Let me know if you change your mind."

Liam's directions took us down a winding country road. When we arrived at the address he had given me, I was surprised to find a tiny house parked on the edge of a patch of bush. The little house was built on a trailer, so it could be moved. But Liam had also attached a small deck to the front.

"Liam lives in a tiny house?" Alice asked. "I had no idea."

"Me either," I said, laughing. The little house was painted bright yellow and had a red tin roof—it was like a child's crayon drawing of a house.

"Look!" Maggie cried. "There's a fort in that tree!"

The tree house looked very much like Liam's tiny house. It was also painted yellow and had a red tin roof. Liam was right when he said the kids would love the house. It was magical.

When he saw us parking the truck, he stepped onto his deck and waved.

"Wow!" said Maggie as she got out of the truck. "Your house is so cute!"

"Thanks!" said Liam, grinning. "Made it myself."

"It's like a kid's playhouse," said Zoe. She tried to sound like she wasn't impressed, but I could tell she was. Excitement lit up her face. Maggie, Zoe and I had often watched TV shows about tiny houses. But we'd never been in one before.

I stepped onto the deck, and Liam's eyes widened as he took in my dress. "Sadie, you look amazing," he said.

"Um, thank you." I felt myself blush.

"Really, you're beautiful. I don't think I've seen you in anything but your work clothes."

"You look nice too." Liam was freshly showered and shaved. He wore clean jeans and a dress shirt. His hair was neatly combed off his face. He almost seemed like a different guy.

"Alice!" Liam said, turning to her. "I didn't expect to see you here today."

Alice glanced at me with an eyebrow raised. "I thought I was invited," she said.

"I asked her to come," I said quickly. "I hope you don't mind, Liam. I thought we'd make an office party of it."

"Sure, sure. That's fine." But he shot me a questioning look. I knew I'd disappointed him.

"Hey, girls!" he said, hugging first Maggie and then Zoe. I held up the bag of brownies for Liam. "I didn't have time to bake my own. Hope these will do." Then I offered him the beers. "And this is to make up for leaving work early on Friday."

Liam laughed and took the six-pack from me. "Apology accepted."

"I brought veggie burgers for myself," said Alice. "We can throw them on the grill with your burgers." She paused. "I hope I'm not the third wheel here."

"No, of course not," he said, glancing at me. "You're welcome to join us. Come on in."

SIX

THE TINY HOUSE was only about three hundred square feet. But the ceiling was high, and there were big windows on each side of the house. Standing outside, you could see right through it. The open floor plan made the house feel big, not tiny.

Alice whistled. "This is beautiful!" she said. "I've never seen anything like it. I had no idea tiny houses could be so—"

"Big?" Liam asked.

She nodded. "It does feel big."

"The light in here is great," I said. "It feels like a mini apartment."

"I love it!" said Maggie, twirling.

"Is that an elevator bed?" Zoe asked Liam. She pointed at a queen-size platform that was hung by metal cords over the couch in the corner.

"An elevator bed?" he asked. "Yes, I guess it is. It goes up and down like an elevator." Liam pushed a button, and the bed lowered.

"I used a garage-door lift to rig this up," he said. "I can lower my bed at night to any level I want. I just put these pins in place, and it stays put. Then I raise the bed up so it's out of the way during the day." He pushed the button again, and the bed rose even higher, nearly to the ceiling.

The couch under the raised bed was a sectional, made of separate pieces that were shoved together. "My boys sleep here when they stay with me," Liam said. "Check this out." He shifted the pieces of the couch around to make two twin-size beds. Then he put the pieces back in place to form an L-shaped couch.

"When you live in a tiny house, everything has to serve more than one purpose." He lifted the foam cushion off the couch to show us. Underneath there was room for storage. He kept blankets and pillows in there.

"You made all this?" I asked, running my finger over the kitchen cupboard.

"I built the couch, the cupboards— everything. And it cost a lot less than you'd think. I used recycled materials wherever I could. Bruce let me take waste wood home from job sites. It was just going to the dump anyway. I bought the rest from a warehouse that sells salvaged building materials."

Maggie danced over to the kitchen at the far end of the house. "Where's your table?" she asked.

"You just walked by it," Liam said. He pulled up two cupboard doors. They hung on hinges, and when they were horizontal they formed a table. Legs folded out from each, like on a card table. "I use this for a desk as well."

"This is so cool!" Zoe said. She was no longer trying to hide her excitement.

The kitchen was small, like what you might find on a boat. But there were lots of cupboards above and below the counter. Liam's bike and skis were hung up high on the wall over the windows. They looked nice up there, like art pieces.

The house was one big room. The only inside door was to the bathroom. And that was at the far end of the house, just beyond the kitchen. Inside the bathroom, Liam had built a small closet for his clothes next to the shower.

"Is this a composting toilet?" I asked.

"Yes. And I have a rain barrel that collects water from the roof for showers and washing. Solar panels on the roof power the place."

"The house is off the grid then," Alice said. "You're not hooked to sewer or electricity."

"And I'm mortgage free." Liam grinned. "I got tired of handing the better part of my paycheck over to a landlord. Now I'm completely out of debt. I've even put a few dollars in the bank. Before I built this place, I was living from check to check, just barely making ends meet."

Alice turned to me. "Maybe this is the answer to your problem," she said. "Build yourself a tiny house." She looked around. "I could live in something like this."

I shook my head. "I couldn't afford it. And it would be too small for the three of us."

"Problem?" Liam glanced from Alice to me. "What problem?"

I sighed. "My landlord is kicking us out so she can rent the place to her daughter."

"You have to move?"

I nodded. "I've been looking everywhere. It's nearly impossible to find a place to rent right now."

"I hope that doesn't mean you're going to leave the area."

I glanced at my daughters. Neither of them wanted to move away. And I didn't want to talk about that possibility now, not with Maggie in the room. She would likely cry and ruin the evening.

Zoe gave me a knowing look. "Come on, Maggie," she said to her sister. "Let's go see that tree fort. I think the grown-ups want to talk."

"It's really cool," Liam told her. "My boys built it. With a little help."

"I built mine too!" Maggie said proudly.

As soon as my girls were outside, Liam

gestured for us to sit on the couch. "Oh, Sadie," he said. "I'm so sorry you're losing your place. That's harsh, especially with the kids."

"I have to find something before the end of the month. But nearly every place I've phoned was already snapped up. And monthly rent is now more than double what I once paid for a mortgage."

"Have you thought about buying another house?"

"I'd like to. I'd much rather pay a mortgage to a bank than rent to a landlord. At least I'd know the money was invested instead of just going out the window. But house prices are so high now. I don't have enough for a down payment in this market."

"Yeah, I know what you mean," said Alice. "When my uncle died, I inherited an acreage. It's outside city limits, so taxes are cheap. But it will be a while before I can afford to build a house on it. That's part of the reason why I took that construction program at the college. I figured I could learn how to build my own home."

"I didn't know you had property," I said.

"It's on a small lake. More like a large pond, really. Pretty though. There are lots of trees. I'll take you and the kids out there before the weather turns. We could pack a picnic. Go for a swim."

"I like that idea," I said. "Buying a piece of land, I mean. And building a house of my own."

I knew exactly what my dream house would look like too. I went on to describe it to Liam and Alice—a house with three bedrooms and an office space for myself. A big kitchen with stainless steel appliances. There had to be at least two bathrooms, so my two daughters weren't always fighting over time in front of the mirror. I *had* to have a great big bathtub to soak in after a day of work. Oh, and a walk-in closet for all those dresses and shoes I hardly ever wore anymore but couldn't bring myself to throw out.

"I used to want a big house like that," said Liam. "But I'm happy with my tiny house now. Living small changes how you think about things."

"What do you mean?" I asked.

He picked up a framed photo of his boys. "Take my kids, for instance. You wouldn't think it, but sharing a small space with my teens brought us closer together." He looked around at the small living area we were sitting in. A flat-screen TV was mounted on the wall to the side. Board games were stacked on the coffee table. "When the boys visit, we're sharing this small space. We're forced to interact, to do things together."

"Huh," I said, thinking of what Alice and I had talked about earlier. "I assumed

I would go batty sharing a space this small with my daughters."

"I thought the same thing," said Liam. "But it didn't turn out that way. My boys and I get along better now than we have in years. I've let go of that dream of a big house. I wouldn't want it even if I could afford it. A big space with lots of rooms puts distance between people."

He put the photo back on the shelf. "But I'll tell you what I *would* like," he said. "I want to run my own construction business. I'm getting tired of working for someone else."

I elbowed him. "You mean, you're getting tired of working for Bruce."

"Maybe." We all laughed.

"So why *don't* you start a business building homes?" I asked. "My dad did. If he hadn't died so young, I imagine I'd be working with him now."

"You've obviously got the skills, Liam," said Alice. She glanced around the tiny house. "What's stopping you?"

"Oh, the usual," said Liam. "Money. It's a big investment to start a construction business."

"Yeah, I'm in the same boat as you two," I said. "I might have the skills to build a house, but I don't have enough money to build it. I'd like to run my own construction business too, like my dad did, but I don't have the money to do that. A nice dream, though, isn't it?"

Liam nodded. "Yeah, a nice dream." And he held my gaze a little too long.

SEVEN

WHEN LIAM GAVE ME that long look, I couldn't turn away. Seeing Liam in his tiny home made me view him in a whole new light. I liked how he saw things, the way he talked about his kids. He didn't care about owning a big house. He wanted to spend time with the people he loved. He seemed so different here than he did at work. I liked what I saw.

Alice cleared her throat to break the moment and remind us she was right there.

Liam and I quickly turned away from each other. Awkward.

"Well," Liam said. "I should get supper started." He grabbed the burgers from the small fridge under the kitchen counter. Then he slipped out to the deck to light the barbecue.

"Liam is full of surprises," I said.

"Yes, he is." Alice shook her head. "I shouldn't have come with you tonight. It's clear Liam wanted you to himself."

"That's exactly why I asked you to join me," I said. "I don't want him to get the wrong idea about us."

"You sure about that?" Alice asked. "It seems to me you like him as much as he likes you."

"I've always *liked* him," I said. "Just not romantically, at least not until—"

"Until?"

"It's just—" I looked around at the tiny house. Liam had more fine carpentry skills than I was aware of. At work we just nailed together walls all day. But he'd built the cabinets and cupboards in this house himself. "Here at home, Liam is way more creative and interesting than he seems at work."

"He certainly has an artist's eye," Alice said. "And I imagine it doesn't hurt that *he* cleans up so nicely."

"You've got that right." I grinned. At work I'd never thought about Liam that way. But here? "Maybe I *can* see myself with him."

"Go talk to him," said Alice. "Let him know you're interested."

"But the kids—"

"I'll keep the kids busy," she said.

She grabbed two beers from the six-pack I'd brought and put them in my hands. "Go talk to him. Now."

"Okay, okay."

Alice gave me a last stern look before leaving the tiny house. She headed out back to the tree fort to hang with the kids.

I found a bottle opener in the kitchen and uncapped the beers before taking them out to Liam. "It's a great house," I said, handing him a beer.

"Thanks."

"No, really. I love the layout. With the high ceiling, it doesn't feel cramped at all. And how you've used every nook and cranny for storage space is really smart."

Liam put the burgers on and closed the barbecue lid. "The best part about building this house was getting my kids involved," he said. "They worked with me during every visit."

He took a swig from his beer. "They grumbled at first but really got into it. We took about five months to build the place. If I'd been working on it fulltime, we could have finished it in two months."

"Huh." I thought about that. I could

throw together a tiny house during the winter season, when we worked less. It would be tough hammering away on my tiny house after a day on the job, but I could do it. "Who knows?" I said. "Maybe this *is* the solution to my housing crisis."

Liam shook his head. "I'm not so sure about that. I've had a hard time finding a place to park this thing. Trailer parks won't take my tiny house because it doesn't fit park standards. They want a sewage tank. And the municipality doesn't see it as a real house because it's so small and doesn't hook into sewer and power."

I laughed, as I was familiar with building and zoning codes. "I imagine the city doesn't know what to do with tiny homes."

"That's an understatement. The bylaws weren't written for them." He lifted his beer at the house behind us. "A buddy let me park it here on his land for the moment. But he wants me out in the spring, as being here isn't exactly legal. I expect town officials will kick me off this property at any time. I'm not sure where I'll go if they do."

"I guess *that* idea is out then," I said. "No tiny house for me." I sighed. "I really don't know what I'm going to do. There just aren't any places to rent that I can afford."

"Yeah, I hear it's bad out there," said Liam. "One of my friends had to move to another city. He couldn't find a place to rent here. And he's single, with no kids."

"I've heard that from parents at Maggie's school too. Families are leaving town because there's no affordable housing here."

"But *you're* not thinking of moving, are you?" Liam asked again.

"I don't want to. The kids grew up here. All their friends are here. And I like my job."

"Even with Bruce for a boss?"

I laughed. "I could do without him.

But I like the rest of the crew." I smiled at him.

Liam blushed. "I'd sure hate to see you go," he said.

I pulled my gaze away. "Look, Liam—"

He took a step back, holding out both hands. "It's okay," he said. "I understand. You brought Alice so I'd get the message that this isn't a date. You're not interested in me."

"You're great, Liam. And the more I see of you in your home, the more I like you. But I admit I felt awkward when you asked me over for dinner. I wasn't sure what to think. We work so well together. I guess I didn't want to jinx that."

"I doubt going on a date would bring us bad luck."

"But if things didn't work out, framing together would be tough."

"Maybe you're overthinking," he said. "We're both grown up enough to figure that one out. I am anyway." He grinned at his small joke.

"I don't know. Maybe you have nothing to do with it."

"I beg your pardon?"

"I mean, maybe I'm just scared." I fiddled with my beer bottle. "My marriage ended when my husband had an affair with a woman he worked with. I felt hurt over that for a long time. I still do."

"I'm so sorry," Liam said.

"And it's been a long time since I've been out on a date. I haven't seen anyone since my divorce. I've just been so focused on making a new life for myself and the girls."

Liam nodded. "When my ex moved away with the boys, I worried I'd never see my kids. I stopped having any kind of a social life. I spent my off time driving to see my boys or bringing them here. That's all I was—Dad."

That about summed up my life too,

I thought. I was *Mom*. When I wasn't at work, I was ferrying my kids around or running the house. There was little time for anything else.

Liam put down his beer and took my hand. "If you're not into starting a new relationship right now, that's okay. I'll be sad for a while, but I'm a big boy. It's not going to get in the way of us working together."

"And if I *am* interested?" I asked.

"Then I think we may have something here. You and I click together, you know?"

I nodded. I knew what he was talking about. Almost from the first day we'd worked together, I'd felt comfortable around Liam. Like I'd always known him. Maybe it was because he reminded me of my dad. Liam was solid. Dependable. Skilled. And he had a great smile.

I squeezed his hand and let go. "Listen, Liam, I have to find a place for me and the kids. I can't think about anything else right now. Once I get that out of the way, we'll go out to dinner and see what happens. Okay?"

"Okay." He opened the barbecue lid and flipped the burgers. "Just hurry up and find a place to live, all right? I don't want to wait too long for that date."

I laughed. "All right. I will!"

EIGHT

I PROMISED NOT only Liam but also my kids that I'd find a place to rent quickly. But at the end of September, I was no closer to finding us a home. Every morning I phoned about the rentals listed in the local paper and online. But most cost more than I could afford. The rest either didn't take kids or had already been snapped up.

Every evening I checked out the few places that were available, but most were too small. In many cases, the girls and I would have had to share a bedroom. The one-bedroom suites were the only rentals I could afford, and even they were overpriced.

So when Alice told me about a two-bedroom basement suite going cheap, I jumped on it. I took the girls along to see the place right after work.

"The basement suite is in town?" Maggie asked as we drove to see it.

"Yes," I said.

"But I don't want to move into town. We talked about that."

"I know, honey. But we're running out of time. We need to move out of our house this weekend."

"I don't want to leave my school."

"Stop whining," said Zoe. "We need a place to live, don't we?"

"It's okay for you," said Maggie. "Your school is in town. Your *boyfriend* is in town. You *want* to move there."

"I don't want to move at all," said Zoe. "I'm sick of moving."

"Both of you be quiet!" I demanded. "Stop arguing."

Zoe slumped in her seat. I glanced in the rearview mirror to see Maggie wiping tears from her eyes. I hated this. Trying to find a place to live was hard on both of my daughters. It was hard on me too.

We drove in silence until we reached the place. The street was in a poorer neighborhood that was literally across the tracks. It was near the town's sewage-treatment plant. I could smell the foul odor of sewage in the air.

"You sure this is the place?" Zoe asked. She peered out the truck window at the old house. The siding hadn't been painted in years. The lawn hadn't been mown in a while either.

"It's the address Alice gave me," I said.

"You phoned ahead, right?"

"Of course," I said.

We walked into the small, unkempt yard, and a woman opened the front door.

"Mrs. Phillips?" I asked.

"You're Alice's friend?"

"Yes," I said, holding out my hand. "I'm Sadie. These are my daughters, Maggie and Zoe."

Mrs. Phillips didn't bother to say hello to the girls. "Come this way. The basement entrance is around back."

We followed her. She unlocked the basement door and let us inside.

"I don't want to live here," Zoe said. "It's too dark." She sniffed. "And it stinks."

"Zoe, please," I said.

"It's a basement suite," the woman said. "They always smell funny."

"It smells like pee!" said Maggie.

Mrs. Phillips gave my kids the once-over.

"Are your kids always this rude?" she asked me.

"I'm sorry," I said. "It's been stressful trying to find a place." I frowned at the girls. "They usually behave themselves."

"Three of you, eh?" Mrs. Phillips said. "There's just the two bedrooms, you know."

"We'll have to *share* a room?" Zoe asked.

"I can share with Maggie," I said.

"But I want my own room too," said Maggie.

Mrs. Phillips pursed her lips. "If the number of bedrooms is a problem, I've got plenty of others interested in the suite."

"It won't be a problem," I said. I eyed the girls, warning them to be quiet.

"If you want the place, I'll need a check for the damage deposit and first month's rent today," said Mrs. Phillips. "And no pets."

"No pets?" cried Maggie. "What are we going to do with Mr. Snuggles?"

"You said we would *never* get rid of our cat," said Zoe. "He's family."

"Of course we won't," I said. I looked back at the woman. "Can't you make an exception? I'm happy to pay a pet deposit."

The woman shook her head. "That's what the last tenant said. But now I have stains on this carpet. As your kid pointed out, you can smell the cat pee. And the former tenant's cat scratched the door. That creature was yowling at all hours of the day and night." She crossed her arms. "No pets."

I turned to the girls. "Maybe we can find someone to take care of Mr. Snuggles for a little while. Just until we find another place. I'm sure Alice wouldn't mind—"

"Hang on a minute," said Mrs. Phillips. "If you're not going to stay, I don't have any interest in renting to you. This isn't a flophouse, you know."

"I didn't mean we would just leave."

I looked between Mrs. Phillips and my girls, feeling trapped. "I just meant—"

"I have half a dozen people lined up to see the place this evening," the woman said. "My phone's been ringing nonstop. Seems like everybody is hunting for a place to rent. I can pick and choose who I want. And I don't want you."

"Surely we can come to an arrangement," I said. "I can pay three months' rent in advance, if you like."

Maggie pulled on my coat sleeve. "I don't want to live here, Mommy."

"Me neither," said Zoe.

"Like I said, I won't be renting to you," the woman said. "Better find yourself another place."

"But—"

She walked back to the door and waited by it until all three of us had filed out. Then she locked the door from the outside.

I nodded at Mrs. Phillips. "Thanks for your time," I told her. She only grunted in return.

I led the kids back to the truck. The smell of the outside air wasn't much better than the odor inside the suite. Everything here smelled like sewage.

Maggie climbed into the back and Zoe sat in the front with me. For a time, I sat still, holding on to the steering wheel with both hands.

"Are we just going to *sit* here?" Zoe said. "This place stinks."

"Don't talk to Mom like that," said Maggie.

"Well, are we?"

"I just need a minute," I said.

"I want to get home," said Zoe. "I've got things to do."

I slapped the steering wheel. "We don't have a home," I said. "Don't you see?

That basement suite was our last option. There are no other places to rent. And we have to move out this weekend."

"Where are we going to live?" Maggie asked. Her lower lip trembled.

"I don't know," I said.

"There must be some other place we can check out," said Zoe. "What about that great house we all liked on Wilson Street? The one with the cool office in the attic."

"I liked that place," said Maggie. "Let's live there!"

"The rent is way too high," I said. "If we lived there, I couldn't afford to pay utilities or buy food. The rent would use up almost my whole paycheck. I'd have nothing left."

"What about that condo?"

"It's already taken," I said. "I've checked out all the places we can afford. Now we're out of time." I turned to Zoe. "You just had to make an issue out of the cat, didn't you?"

Zoe blinked away tears.

"I'm sorry, Mommy," Maggie said from the back seat. "I didn't mean to mess things up. But we can't leave Mr. Snuggles behind."

I took a deep breath, willing my anger away. "Neither of you is to blame. This one's on me. I just don't know what to do. We need to move out this weekend, and we have no place to go."

"You're not going to move us to a different town, right?" said Zoe. "I mean, all my friends are here. I know kids who've moved away because their parents couldn't find a place—"

I shook my head. "We're not moving to another town. I won't make you leave your friends. My work is here." I reached back and took Maggie's hand. "And we're not getting rid of Mr. Snuggles."

"What are we going to do?" Zoe asked.

I glanced up the street, trying to think

of an answer. The street was lined with one house after another. Why couldn't I find a home for us? Then I spotted a motorhome parked in someone's driveway.

"I know what we're going to do," I said. I started up the truck and pulled out into the street. "We're going camping."

NINE

I DROVE our travel trailer to a campground just down the road from Maggie's school. It was one of those places with both an older motel and campsites on the same property. It being the end of September, there were lots of sites available. I booked the largest they had, nestled between trees for privacy.

I backed the trailer into the spot and turned off the truck engine. "There," I said. "Isn't this a great spot?"

Zoe hunkered down in the truck seat and

started biting her nails. "This is so embarrassing," she said.

"It'll be fun," I said. "We're *camping.* You always liked camping."

"Not when the travel trailer is our *home.*"

"I think it's cool," said Maggie. "It's like we're on vacation. Isn't that right, Mr. Snuggles?" She hugged our cat. He'd yowled in panic all the way here.

"This isn't a holiday," said Zoe. "We're at school, stupid. And Monday is October first. It's fall, not summer."

"Don't call your sister stupid," I said.

"Whatever."

I checked my temper. The last thing I wanted right now was another argument. Zoe's behavior was getting worse. But I knew she was only acting like this because she was upset. We were all unsettled at losing our house.

I tried to put a positive spin on things.

"We're so close to Maggie's school," I said. "It's just a five-minute walk. Zoe, you can take Maggie to school and catch the bus into town from there."

"What if my friends see us leaving the campsite every morning?" Zoe asked. "They will, you know. The buses drive right by here. I don't want them to know I live in a travel trailer parked at a campsite."

"It's only for the month," I said. "Not even that, if we're lucky. I'll find a place for November."

"You said we'd have a place by *now*."

I put a hand on her arm to comfort her. "Listen, I know living here for the month embarrasses you. It embarrasses me too. I never thought I'd be in this position."

"Homeless, you mean?" said Zoe.

I felt my stomach drop.

"We're *not* homeless," Maggie said. "We've got a travel trailer. We're camping."

"That's the spirit," I said. "Let's make this fun."

But we *were* homeless—or nearly homeless. I suddenly worried that school staff or social workers might look on our living situation as child neglect. Could I lose my kids because we'd moved into our trailer?

"How about we keep this to ourselves for now," I said. "We don't need to let your dad or your teachers know we're camping. We'll just pretend we're still living at our rented house."

"You want us to lie to Dad?" Maggie said, surprised. "You told us we shouldn't lie."

"We'll tell him we're moving when we find our new place. Okay?"

"Okay." Maggie sounded doubtful.

Zoe didn't say anything to that. She just scowled at me and turned away. But then, I thought, she *should* be mad. I *had* just asked my daughters to lie to their dad about living at the campsite. How had I gotten to this place?

"Where are we going to put all our stuff?" Maggie asked.

"We'll have to get rid of a lot," I said.

"I'm not giving up my stuffies," said Maggie.

"And I'm not giving up my books," said Zoe.

"I'll rent a storage unit," I said. "We can put our furniture and other items in there. But we'll also have to take a load to the thrift store today."

Zoe sighed in disgust. "I already gave up a pile of stuff when we lost our house after you guys got divorced."

"You had outgrown most of those things," I reminded her. "And you've outgrown a lot of things in your room now. Think how happy some kid will be to find those toys and books at the thrift store."

"But it's *my* stuff."

"I wouldn't mind giving my Barbie dolls to another girl," said Maggie. "If it made her happy."

"Well, I'm not giving away *my* things," said Zoe.

"You *will* have to get rid of some of it," I said. "I will too."

"Like all those dresses in your closet that you hardly ever wear?" Zoe asked. She meant it as a gibe, but I let it go. She was right. I rarely wore them.

I nodded. "Many of them, yes." I wasn't quite sure why I had hung on to them. My life had changed so much since my divorce. Now I wore jeans, T-shirts and work boots most of the time.

But maybe I would hang on to a couple of those dresses. Once I finally found a place, I had at least one date coming up with Liam.

I smiled at the thought. Then I shook my head. I was getting ahead of myself. I had to find a home for my kids first.

"Zoe, I know this is hard. But things will turn around. We'll find a place. We'll get settled. It will all work out. You'll see. And in the meantime, we're camping! You love camping!"

"I *used* to love camping," said Zoe. "When I was a kid."

"And you're *so* grown up now," said Maggie.

"I'm fourteen," said Zoe. "That's a lot older than you."

"She thinks she's so grown up because she's got a *boyfriend*."

"Shut up. Do not."

"When am I going to meet this Jason?" I asked.

"Like, *never*," said Zoe. "I'm not inviting him over to our *travel trailer*." Then she muttered under her breath, "I should have gone to live with Dad when he offered."

"You don't mean that," I said.

"He's got a nice house, and he lives in the city. We're stuck out here in the middle of nowhere. And you're moving us into a travel trailer on a *campsite!*"

"You told me you didn't want to leave the area. Your friends are here. You *begged* me not to move!"

Caught, she shook her head a little. "Well, maybe I was wrong. Anything is better than living at a *campsite.*"

Maggie put her hands over her ears. "I hate it when you guys argue!" she shouted.

I sighed. "Maggie's right. We're stressed right now. But there's no need to take it out on each other."

Zoe shrugged and looked away, but she didn't say anything more. She was a good kid in a bad place. I understood why she was angry.

"We're here at the campsite for now," I said. "We might as well make the best of it. Let's cook on the barbecue every night, and roast marshmallows over the fire pit. It will be like the old days."

"You mean the old days when we used to camp with Dad?" Zoe asked.

I nodded haltingly. "Sure. Like back then."

"It won't be like that," said Zoe. "It will never be like that again."

"I know," I said. "But we'll still have fun. Lately we've all been living our separate lives. In the evenings you and Maggie have been on your phones and laptops. I don't spend as much time with you as I'd like. Camping in the travel trailer will give us a chance to get closer."

"I don't want to get *closer*," Zoe said. "I want my own space."

God, I do too, I thought. But I kept my

mouth shut. We just had to find a way to make this work until I found a place. I was out of options.

"Do they even have Wi-Fi here?" Zoe asked.

"At the motel but not out on the grounds," I admitted.

"Argh!" Zoe jumped out of the truck and stormed into the trailer. She slammed the flimsy trailer door behind her.

Maggie leaned over the seat of the crew cab and wrapped her arms around my neck. "It will be okay, Mommy," she said.

I patted her arm. "I know, honey. Camping here is only temporary." But after nearly a month of searching for a place, I just wasn't sure of that anymore.

TEN

I KEPT SEARCHING for a place to rent for the next couple of weeks. But by mid-October we still lived at the campground. I thought maybe now that the summer people had gone, I could at least find a cabin to rent. I was surprised to find most of the tourists who owned cabins in the area didn't rent them out for the winter.

Desperate, I started looking at the more expensive rentals. If I used the little bit of money I'd socked away from the sale of our house the year before, I could rent one of these high-priced houses. But I quickly realized that if I did, that money would be gone in just a few months. I'd have nothing to show for it. And then we would have to move out again. We'd be right back where we'd started.

I was fretting over the problem at work when I banged my finger with a hammer. I swore as I nursed the wound.

"You okay there, Sadie?" Liam asked. He put down his framing nailer and came over to me. "You seem out of sorts."

"Yeah, I'm fine," I said, still holding the hurt finger. "I'm just angry with myself. I've been doing dumb things like that all week."

"It's stress," said Liam. "It makes you clumsy and forgetful. You need a break." He grinned. "How about we finally go out on that date?"

I shook my head. "I'm sorry, Liam. Not yet. I need every spare moment outside work to hunt down a place to rent. And I'm beginning to doubt I'll ever find anything. Even the crappy basement suites are out of my price range now. It's getting too cold to camp out in the travel trailer. I think it's time I started looking for a place to rent in another community."

Liam appeared alarmed. "But will you find work at this time of year? Winter is almost on us. Construction is about to slow down. Will you even find a new job before spring?"

"I don't know. But what else can I do? If I can't find a home for my kids here, then I've got to consider living in other areas."

Liam took my sore finger in his hand and inspected it. Then, to my surprise, he kissed the bruised knuckle. "I don't want you to leave," he said, holding my hand. "I know I have no claim on you. Not yet. But I don't want to lose you."

I was stunned by his words but flattered too. I felt a spark of excitement surge through me. "I don't want to leave either," I said. I smiled up at him. "Especially now."

Liam leaned forward like he was about to kiss me, right here in this unfinished house. But then our crew boss yelled at us. "Hey!" Bruce said. "You two lovebirds make out on your own time. Right now you're on the clock."

I quickly pulled my hand from Liam's. Our crew boss had heard and seen everything. But of course he would have. We were on a new building site, with only the wall frames between us. Could this day get any worse?

Then my phone buzzed, announcing a call. "*Shit*," I said under my breath when I saw who it was.

"Zoe causing trouble again?" Liam asked.

I shook my head. "My ex-husband, Kevin."

"Oh." Liam stepped away.

I turned my back on him as I answered the phone. "I'm working," I told Kevin. "Can't this wait?"

"I don't think it can," Kevin said. "Zoe just called, and she was really upset, crying. She said you and the girls are living in the travel trailer at a campsite."

I closed my eyes for a moment. I had worried Zoe would tell him. "Only for now," I said. "Until I can find a place to rent. There's a housing crisis here."

"It hardly sounds short-term. Zoe says you've been looking for a place all over and haven't found anything. That travel trailer you're staying in leaks, and it's not insulated. What are you going to do when winter hits? That's only a few weeks away."

"I'll find a place before then." I have to, I thought.

"But you just said there's a housing crisis."

"Kevin, I'm doing the best I can. I spend every hour I'm not working trying to track down a house to rent."

"What are you going to do? You can't raise our daughters in a travel trailer. That's one step up from homelessness."

There was that word again. We *were* nearly homeless. How had I let this happen?

"I'll find something," I said.

"Until you do, I think the girls should come live with me."

"No!" I cried, louder than I'd intended. I glanced at Liam and lowered my voice. "They are not going to live with you."

"Liz and I have more than enough room in my house," Kevin said. "The girls can each have their own bedroom."

Liz? I felt anger well up inside. "That woman broke up our home. She's the reason we had to sell our house in the first place. She is not going to raise my girls."

"Liz didn't break up our home, and you know it," said Kevin. "Our marriage was over long before that."

I glanced at Liam. He'd overheard everything I'd just said. But then, Bruce had too. I lowered my voice further. "I don't want to argue about that," I told Kevin. "It's in the past. But I'm not giving up the girls. They live with me."

"You may have no choice."

"What do you mean?"

"You clearly can't take care of them," he said.

I tried to keep my voice level. "I'm *not* neglecting my children."

"Sadie, they are living in a travel trailer at a campsite. You aren't providing them with a decent home."

I felt my chin tremble with emotion.

"You have no right to tell me I'm not taking care of my kids. I'm a good mom. I'm always there for them. You only see them a few times a year, on holidays."

Kevin didn't respond to that taunt. Instead he softened his voice. "Zoe is scared, Sadie. And she's ashamed at how you're living. Do you really want her to feel like that?"

"Does Zoe want to live with you?"

Kevin paused. "I don't know. We didn't get to that. I wanted to talk to you first. She phoned to ask for my help. She wanted to know if I could send more child support, so you could afford a place to rent."

I covered my mouth. "Oh, god." I was shocked Zoe felt she had to do that. But she was trying to help me, in her way.

"I'll talk to her," I said. "I'll explain she shouldn't have done that."

"You can't expect the girls to keep living like this, Sadie. It's not fair to them. Either find a place there or move to another town where you *can* find a place to rent. I expect you to put a roof over their heads right away. By this weekend. Otherwise, I want the girls to come live with me. If you fight me on that, I'll take you to court."

"Kevin, please don't do this."

"I'm only thinking about what's best for our daughters."

"*Please*, Kevin."

"I have to go. We'll talk more about this." Then he hung up on me.

I stared at the phone in disbelief. This couldn't be happening, I thought. I couldn't lose my girls. I just *couldn't*.

When Liam saw how upset I was, he held me by both shoulders. "What's going on?" he asked, even though I was sure he'd heard nearly everything.

"My ex found out we were living at the campsite."

"Zoe told him?" Liam asked.

I nodded. "Since we don't have a house, he wants the girls to live with him. He's threatening to go to court if he needs to."

Liam took me in his arms. "I'm so sorry, Sadie."

I saw Bruce frown at us, but he also turned away to allow us some privacy. He clearly knew how hard this was for me.

I pulled away from Liam and ran both hands over my head. "My ex is right, isn't he? I've let my girls down."

"No, you haven't," Liam said. "You did everything you could to find a home for your kids. There's just nothing out there. At least, nothing most of us can afford. We need to build more affordable housing in this community."

"I don't want the girls to live with Kevin. But am I just being selfish? Maybe it's best if the girls stay with their father for now. Just until I sort things out."

"You know how that goes," he said. "If the girls are living with your ex, he's got them. A judge won't want to move the girls again unnecessarily. In any case, once the kids are established in a new school, are they really going to want to leave?"

I knew Liam was talking about his own story. I doubted his boys would ever live with him full-time again. The thought of losing my own girls made my eyes sting with tears. But was that what Zoe really wanted, to live with her dad? I had to find that out right away.

ELEVEN

"CAN YOU GIVE me a moment?" I asked Liam. I kept my head down as I headed toward the portable toilets. I hoped to avoid talking to my crew boss. But Bruce called out anyway.

"You're not leaving *again*, are you?" he asked.

"No," I said, trying to control my tears. "I'm just going to the bathroom."

But the stinky portable toilet on the job site was the last place I wanted to go. I hid behind it instead, taking a moment to control my emotions. Then I pulled out my phone, pressed Zoe's name on my contact list and waited for her to answer.

"*What?*" she asked. No hello. She knew it was me calling.

"Are you in class?" I asked.

"No. It's my spare."

"Good. We need to talk."

"What about?" she asked.

"I think you know. I just got a call from your father."

"Yeah, so?"

"He said you told him we were living at a campsite."

"We *are*."

"I know, honey," I said quietly. For a moment I didn't know what else to say.

"Is that it?" she asked. "Can I go now?"

I was taken aback by the anger in her voice. "No," I said firmly. "We have a few things to discuss."

"Like what?"

"For starters, why now? Why didn't you phone your dad when we first moved to the campsite?"

"You told us not to."

Like that ever stopped you, I thought. "I mean, your dad said you seemed really upset when you called him."

"Of course I'm freaked out. We don't have a place to live."

"Something else is going on here, Zoe. I know you. What's happened?"

She paused so long I thought she'd hung up.

"You still there, Zoe?" I asked.

"I just broke up with Jason, okay?"

Broke up? But she'd only known him since school started. "I'm sorry, Zoe," I said. I pinched my nose in frustration. "But I don't see the connection. Why would you phone your dad about our living situation after breaking up with your boyfriend?"

"One of Jason's friends told him we live at the campsite. The guy saw Maggie and me getting out of the travel trailer this morning. Jason thought that was hilarious. I mean, he made fun of me, Mom. He made fun of our family for living like that." Her voice cracked with emotion. "So I ended things."

"Oh, honey."

I could hear her crying over the phone. I just wanted to hold her. Of course my ex was right. Living at the campsite wasn't fair to either of my girls.

I sighed. "Your dad wants you and Maggie to live with him. Is that what you want?"

"I want to live in a *house*."

"Do you want to move in with your dad and Liz?"

"No! I don't want to move away from here. I don't want to leave you. I just—I thought maybe Dad could give you more money so we could afford a place."

"I know. He told me." I hesitated. "If you *do* want to move in with him, then I can make it happen." I chose my words carefully. "But please understand I want you here. With me."

"If we can find a place to rent right away. Otherwise…" Zoe trailed off.

I understood. She would stay if I could find a place *now*. If not, she wanted to live with Kevin.

I glanced back at the job site. Together our crew could build a house in just a few months. Why couldn't I provide a home for my daughters? Money, I thought. That was the problem. I couldn't afford to build a house or even buy the land to put it on.

Then I caught sight of the guesthouse we were building to the side of the job site. It was about the size of Liam's tiny house, three hundred square feet. We'd roughed out the shell of that cabin in no time at all. Maybe

I *could* put a roof over my daughters' heads.

"Okay, honey," I told Zoe. "I'll deal with this. One way or another, we'll be out of that campsite by the end of the week."

"This week? Promise?"

"I promise."

"Where are we going to go?"

"I have an idea, but I need to work a few things out first. I'll tell you about it later, okay?"

"Mom?"

"Yes, honey?"

"Parts of living at the campsite are okay," she said. "The evenings are nice. I like playing games and talking around the campfire. We used to hang out like that after I got home from school, remember? I could tell you stuff. Then, after you and Dad split up…"

She didn't finish, but I knew what she meant. After I'd started working again and we moved to the rental, we rushed to have supper, do chores and homework. Then the girls disappeared into their rooms to scan the net or stream movies while I watched TV. We didn't do much together anymore.

Alice rounded the corner of the portable outhouse. "Bruce told me to find you," she said. "He wants you to get back to work."

I nodded at Alice as I wrapped up my call with Zoe. She started to leave, but I waved her back so I could talk to her.

"I've got to go," I told Zoe. "Talk later?"

"Later," she said.

We ended the call.

"What's going on?" Alice asked. "You look wrecked."

"A few weeks ago you said I could stay with you. Is that offer still open?"

"Of course."

"Can I move in this weekend?"

"I don't see why not. I'll have to clean

out my office first. But that should only take a couple of hours. You could even move in tonight, if you wanted."

"I'll help you pay your rent for as long as we're staying with you."

"You bet you will!" she said. "You're not the only one facing a higher cost of living, you know. My rent went way up over the last year. Almost half of my paycheck goes to rent now. No one can afford to live like that."

"Are you sure about this, Alice? I expect we'll be there for a few months."

"As long as you and the girls do most of the cooking and cleaning."

I laughed in relief. "You're on. Okay, now I've got something else I want to talk to you and Liam about."

"What is it?" she asked as she followed me back to the unfinished house.

I held up a hand to get her to wait a moment. Liam stood upright and wiped his brow as we reached him. I took a deep breath and launched right in.

"I need a place to live," I said. "You need a spot to park your tiny house. And Alice, you can't afford to build a house on your land."

"Yeah, so?"

"I don't have an easy fix for our problems," I said. "But I may have an idea of how we can help each other out."

I turned back to Liam. "How would you like to help me build a tiny house?"

Liam shrugged. "Sure. I'm game. I had a blast building mine."

"How about you, Alice?"

"I guess. Yeah, that could be fun. I'm sure I'd learn a lot from you two."

"I can't afford to pay either of you," I said.

Liam laughed. "I knew there was a catch."

"In fact, I'm hoping to build on the

cheap," I said. "I was thinking about taking apart our old camper and using the trailer from that as the foundation of my tiny house."

"That might work," Liam said, considering the idea. "And like I said, we can use recycled materials." Then he scratched his cheek. "But once we build the tiny house, where are you going to park it? You don't want the city chasing you off a property because you aren't legal."

"Maybe I'll put my tiny house the same place you'll put yours?" I glanced sideways at Alice.

"You want to park your tiny house on my property?" Alice asked.

I nodded. "Not only that, I'd like to build *your* tiny house there too. But maybe we can put yours on a permanent foundation."

Alice's face lit up. "You'd do that? You'd help me build my own tiny house?"

"Liam and I would trade our skills and labor for a place to park our tiny homes rent free. For a given period of time," I added. "We can work out details and write up a contract. My dad always said contracts keep friends friendly."

"But can we get the approval to do that?" Liam asked. "Tiny houses don't exactly fit building and zoning codes."

"Yes, but Alice's place is outside the city limits, which may make things easier. And we'll apply for temporary permits before we begin building. After that we'll hammer out details with the district. I'm hoping we can get permission to park there legally and permanently."

"You think that's likely?"

"We'll see. But this is one thing I can do for you in exchange for helping me build. From working for my dad, I've got a pretty good idea how to work with local officials to get a job done. I'll make sure they aren't going to chase us off the property. Alice, what do you think?"

"Sounds good. I'm in." She lifted her chin at Bruce, who glared at us with his hands on his hips. "But for now, I think we better get back to work."

I picked up my nailer and bent over the wall we were working on. When I saw Bruce turn away, I quietly asked Liam, "So how about I come over to your place Sunday? You and I should have that dinner *before* we start building, don't you think? I don't want to wait until next spring for our first date."

Liam laughed. "You're on. But maybe leave the kids and Alice at home this time? Let's make it dinner for just the two of us."

I grinned. "It's a date."

TWELVE

THAT FIRST DATE with Liam wasn't our last. Liam moved his little house to Alice's property. There we spent most evenings working together on my tiny house. When we were alone, we often shared a late supper, lit by candlelight.

But then, we weren't often alone. Alice and the kids usually worked on the tiny house right along with us. The girls and I were also now living with Alice, of course. And Liam, Alice and I worked together for Bruce during the day.

So we all spent a little too much time together as we built my house. So much so that Alice and I started to squabble like sisters. But that was okay. She had become family. My daughters even started calling her auntie.

I can't say staying at Alice's place for those four months was easy. But after living in the travel trailer for a month, her apartment seemed big. And I was surprised at how quickly my view of things had shifted. Before my divorce, I'd thought I needed a big house and a whole lot of things to be happy. Now I was just happy to have a roof over my head.

Getting rid of my stuff was also freeing. When we'd moved into the travel trailer, we had put some furniture in a small storage unit. But the girls and I had gotten rid of most of our extra clothing and other unused things.

As we moved a second time into Alice's apartment, we got rid of even more stuff. I felt like I was finally letting go of my old

GAIL ANDERSON-DARGATZ

life, the one I'd once shared with my ex-
husband, Kevin. Of course, dating Liam
also helped me forget the life I'd left behind.

In the process of downsizing, I realized how few objects I actually needed. At
Alice's place, the girls and I kept only our
laptops and one bag of personal items each.
Everything was tucked away in the one closet
when not in use.

Before, when we had the house, the girls'
bedrooms had been a mess. Toy, books and
clothes were all over the floor. The bedroom
we shared now was uncluttered. I found
this change quite restful. I wasn't fighting
with my daughters all the time—not about
cleaning up, at least.

And sharing a room with the girls was
surprisingly pleasant. Instead of spending
evenings alone in separate rooms as we had
at our rented house, we snuggled up together
on the bed. There we surfed the Web or

watched movies together for a change.

I started to feel connected to my girls again, particularly Zoe. It was strange to think that just sharing a smaller space had brought us closer. I never would have believed that before we lost our rental. I'd assumed that living in close quarters would just lead to arguments. But we had *fewer* arguments now. Liam had been right when he said living small changes things.

By the time our tiny house was finished, even Zoe was used to living in a small space. In fact, at four hundred square feet, the tiny house seemed big in comparison to the bedroom we'd been sharing. And we didn't have much to move. Our things all fit easily into the back of my truck.

Liam and Alice helped us carry our few things into our tiny house as our cat explored our new home. Once we were done putting things away, we cracked open beers to celebrate.

The girls had root beer, of course.

I raised my beer to Liam, Alice and my daughters. "Here's to us!" I said. Then I raised my glass to the house. "We made this!" We all clinked our bottles together. "Thanks, Alice, Liam. I couldn't have done it without you."

"Hell, I'm just glad to be rid of you," said Alice. She grinned as she took a sip, so I knew she was joking. But I also knew she was relieved to have her small apartment to herself.

"What do you think, Zoe?" I asked. "Will you invite friends over now?"

"Are you kidding?" Zoe said. "My friends are *dying* to see this place. I've told them all about it. They're, like, *so* jealous."

I took in a deep, satisfied breath and looked around at the house we had created together. Since the three of us would live in this tiny house, I had decided to make it bigger than Liam's. Our little house had two lofts, one on each end of the building, for the girls. I'd put my bedroom on the ground floor, and we had built Maggie's loft over it.

The bathroom was at the other end of the house, and Zoe's loft was above it. We installed a full bath and shower, so the bathroom was nearly the size of the one in Alice's apartment. Given how much time the girls and I spent in the bathroom, we figured we'd give it more space. But I was also tired of banging on the bathroom door for Zoe to come out. I put a mirror and power in both girls' lofts. Zoe could do her hair and makeup up there.

I also made sure both girls had some privacy. Each loft had a short wall, so I couldn't see up into their rooms from below. All our bedrooms had a small closet and shelves for our clothes.

The center of the house was one large space with high ceilings. I put in big windows on either side of the door. And we painted the walls white to keep that light, airy feeling. The main living area didn't feel small at all.

The kitchen ran along the wall opposite the door in the main room. There was lots of cupboard space above the sink and stove. We bought a small fridge to fit underneath the kitchen counter.

We decided we didn't need a couch, as we no longer had a TV. There really wasn't room for one, in any case. When we wanted to watch a show together on our laptops, we'd just cuddle up on my bed or in one of the girls' lofts.

What we really needed was a good-sized table to work and eat on. That's where we would hang out together. So Liam and I built a table to fit the main living space beside the small kitchen. For seating, we built cubes that could be shoved together to form benches. Each cube also opened for storage.

The stairs leading to each girl's loft had shelves on the sides. But we had let go of so much stuff that we found we didn't need all the storage we'd built into the house.

I took another deep breath and nodded, pleased with our work. I was proud of what we'd accomplished here.

"Look!" Maggie cried. "Mr. Snuggles has found his tree house already!" Our cat had jumped up the stairs to Maggie's loft, then hopped into a box Maggie had built just for him. At Maggie's request, I had installed the box high on the wall. Mr. Snuggles peered out of the box at us from his perch near the ceiling. Maggie climbed the stairs after the cat. "I built that for you, Mr. Snuggles," she said. "I built it all by myself."

Getting the kids to help was the best part of building the tiny house—Liam had been right about that too. Even Zoe had gotten into the project. She had come up with the idea to use a sliver of space between two cupboards for a pull-out spice rack. With my instruction, she had put it together herself.

"Building this tiny house was fun," said Maggie from her loft. "Can we make another one?"

"We're building Alice's tiny house next," I said. "How about we start next weekend?"

"I'll be so thrilled to get out of that apartment and into my own home," Alice said. "Especially if it's anything like this one. Wow."

"I'm with Maggie," said Liam. "Building a tiny house *is* fun, way more fun than building a regular house. There are more challenges. I like coming up with cool ways to make use of space."

"Do you like it enough to make a business out of it?" I asked Liam.

"What do you mean?"

I turned to Alice. "We build your house next. But let's make it a real showcase home, to show customers what we can do. Then we start building them for others."

"You're talking about starting a construction company," Alice said, "to build tiny homes."

"Yes. We would start small." I grinned. "No pun intended. And build the business over time. Down the road, I'd like to buy some land and offer clients a place to park their homes."

Alice held her chin as she thought about the idea. "So like a trailer park, but for tiny houses."

"Exactly. A micro village. It would take some time to go through the process of getting approval, of course. We'd want to get the community onside."

"It's going to take a lot of work, getting a construction business going," said Liam.

"Of course it will. But my own dad built his from the ground up. I know we can too.

Look what we've done already."

"That *has* always been a dream of mine," said Liam. "To own a construction business so I don't have to work for someone else."

"Yes! And keeping the business small means we can work at a sane pace. Living tiny, we can afford to work less. I want to be around for my kids a whole lot more."

"And I could build too," said Maggie.

"Yes, you could!" I said.

"I wouldn't mind helping out," Zoe said. She shrugged. "If you paid me."

I turned to her, surprised and delighted. I had started working for my dad when I was her age. "I'd love that," I said.

Alice rubbed her hands together. "Okay, let's do it."

Liam lifted his beer. "Here's to making our dreams a reality."

I clicked my beer with his. "I'll drink to that," I said.

AUTHOR'S NOTE

The idea for this short novel began when my daughter Hadarah brought home her school's tiny-house project. Her task was to come up with a tiny-house floor plan and design her own tiny home. We watched TV shows on tiny houses, and I became intrigued by the idea of letting go of the stuff that clutters our lives, living simply and within a cozy space.

Tiny houses really *are* tiny, between sixty and four hundred square feet. And they are often built on trailers, so they can be moved from place to place. It's like camping with a travel trailer, only better. You get to live in a home that feels like a real house.

Tiny homes are also a great way to go green. Building and living in them uses fewer resources. Many tiny homes are heated and powered by solar panels. And, of course, they *cost less* to build and live in. Many tiny-house owners say they pay no mortgage and are no longer in debt. At a time when people struggle to pay for or even find a home, the tiny house seems like a solution to the housing crisis.

As I wrote this book, I looked into the housing crisis within my own province. What I found was troubling. Families are living at campsites because they can't find affordable places to rent. And these are families in which both adults are holding down decent jobs. It's a situation that's mirrored in other parts of the country.

Of course, homelessness is an ongoing tragedy. People are living on the streets without shelter, very often through cold winters. Others end up couch surfing. And the people who find themselves in this situation are often the most vulnerable members of our community: mothers with children, the mentally ill and the elderly.

Is the tiny-house movement a solution to homelessness and the housing crisis? Perhaps. Communities are beginning to consider that possibility. Check out the Dignity Village project in Portland, Oregon. Similar tiny-house villages have popped up in other west-coast cities.

Tiny-house ownership is not without problems though. Municipalities often don't allow tiny houses, as they don't fit current building and zoning regulations. Many people build tiny homes but can't find a place to park them.

Yet cities are beginning to rethink bylaws to accommodate tiny homes. "Micro villages" are starting to pop up, often outside city limits. Bluegrass Meadows Micro Village outside Terrace, British Columbia, is an example.

Will I ever live in a tiny home? I'm married

to a carpenter, who has the skills to build one. And we've talked about it. The reality is that we already live in a small home and are happy with it. Still, I find the idea of living in a tiny house appealing—a cozy home off the grid that we could move from place to place. Leaving less of an environmental footprint. And no mortgage to worry about! Living with less, so we could work less. Now that's a life!

ACKNOWLEDGMENTS

I'm grateful to my lovely daughter Hadarah for introducing me to the tiny-house movement and inspiring me to dig deeper into the subject. As always, I'd like to thank my editor, Ruth Linka, and Orca Book Publishers for their commitment to literacy through the Rapid Reads program. I'm proud to be a Rapid Reads author.

If you're interested in learning more about building or buying a tiny house, I found the following resources and stories useful as I wrote this short novel.

Tiny Home Alliance Canada has an excellent website that includes a section called "Process Tips" for building your own tiny home. The Tiny House Festival site has a page called "Tiny House Bylaws in Canada" that outlines common issues and offers a list of communities that welcome tiny houses.

I was delighted to see that a great many women are building their own tiny homes. Google the topic and you'll see what I mean. Kayla Feenstra of Abbotsford, British Columbia, is one example. She built her tiny house for just $15,000. Like other women, she went on to start her own tiny-house construction business. Hers is called Tiny Homes Canada. You'll find a "Tiny House 101" primer on the Tiny Homes Canada site.

By the age of eighteen, **GAIL ANDERSON-DARGATZ** knew she wanted to write about women in rural settings. Today Gail is a bestselling author. *A Recipe for Bees* and *The Cure for Death by Lightning* were finalists for the Scotiabank Giller Prize. She also teaches other authors how to write fiction. Gail divides her time between the Shuswap region of British Columbia and Manitoulin Island in Ontario. For more information, visit gailanderson-dargatz.ca.